Adorning The Empress

Published by:
FormAsia Books Limited
706 Yu Yuet Lai Building
45 Wyndham Street
Central, Hong Kong
www.formasiabooks.com

Published 2002
Reprint 2004
ISBN: 962-7283-85-1

Written by May Holdsworth
Proofread by M.K. Shankar
Designed by Format Limited
Photography by FormAsia Books/Kwan Kwong Chung
Camera Assistant: Sathish Gobinath
FormAsia Marketing: Eliza Lee

All textiles and accessories from the collection of:
Teresa Coleman Fine Arts Limited, Hong Kong
Honeychurch Antiques, Hong Kong

Theme paintings and portraits by kind permission of:
Martyn Gregory Gallery, London

Printed in China by RR Donnelley
Colour separations by Sky Art Graphic Company Limited, Hong Kong

Adorning The Empress

May Holdsworth

FormAsia

Adorning The Empress

We shall begin with a picture: two Chinese women dressed in coloured silks, their hair entwined with jewels of coral and jade, are standing in a courtyard. They are as slight and exquisite as a pair of butterflies blown by some wind to the edge of a lotus pond. One leans gently against the balustrade, a soft hand on the painted wood. Her eyes are lowered to the pair of mandarin ducks in the blue-grey water that laps beneath her feet. Behind, in the airy hall from which they have emerged, we can see arrayed the decorative trappings of a house of wealth and position: a calligraphy scroll; paintings of peach blossom and of mountains; a cherry-red porcelain vase on a narrow table of polished elm, perhaps, or *huanghuali*; the formal arrangement of a row of high-backed chairs. On the other side of a latticed partition, the man of the house discusses a line in some classical text with a young companion. He has an air of self-consequence; perhaps an important provincial official or a rich landlord, he is master of all he surveys.

The Chinese artist who painted this canvas* probably had his eye on patrons who would buy his daubs, but no less was he illustrating what could be

**A detail of this painting appears on pages 56-57.*

observed around him. Commercial though it might have been, his portrayal of figures and setting was still realistic in evoking a certain tone. It precisely conveyed the blend of sophisticated taste and artifice that graced life within the grand mansions of China's cultivated elite in the Qing dynasty. Characterised by affluence, refinement and seclusion, it was a life brilliantly depicted in the great 18th-century novel, *The Dream of the Red Chamber*.

The book can be read on several levels. At its simplest it is both a romance and a novel of manners. It chronicles the fortunes of the rich and well-connected Jia family from its heyday to its decline. Cao Xueqin, the author, was himself the scion of an aristocratic family which had fallen upon hard times. For three generations members of the Cao family had held high office. As Commissioners of Imperial Textiles, an appointment carrying great influence, they supervised the government-owned silk factories in the Yangtze valley which produced the fabrics and gowns that adorned the imperial court in Beijing. Then they lost the emperor's patronage and Cao Xueqin ended his days in penury. In writing *The Dream of the Red Chamber*, he therefore had the history of his own family to draw from, and what went on in the Jia household was clearly akin to what he had known in his youth.

Such households invariably occupied a series of houses interconnected by courtyards, gardens and passage-ways. These would be built with the rarest hardwoods and decorated in the finest styles. The Jia family mansion was no different. We need only to read one description of the entrance to guess what splendours might be found inside. You enter through an ornamental gate. Within, balustraded loggias running along the sides and a covered passage-way at the centre lead you to a courtyard screened by a slab of polished marble set in a red sandalwood frame. Painted and carved beams and rafters form a picturesque canopy overhead, and the galleries on either side of the courtyard are brightened by the colourful parrots and cockatoos chirping inside their cages under the swooping eaves.

The walls around the spacious grounds enclose a host of characters from the most venerable matriarch to the lowliest servant. This numerous cast is manipulated, like so many puppets in a shadow play, through a luxurious and outwardly decorous domestic existence punctuated by feasts, visits, operas and poetry readings, meetings and partings.

Among the younger members is a granddaughter, Lin Daiyu. A heroine of exaggerated sensibility, she is prone to express her depths of feeling in poetry and frequent recourse to tears. In a scene made famous by its regular inclusion in performances of opera excerpts, she is found grieving over wind-blown peach blossom on a late spring day. We see her at a central location in the novel, among the "rose-crowned pergolas" and "small pavilions embowered in peonies" of Prospect Garden, presiding over the ceremonial burial of fallen flowers and reciting, in between sobs:

"One day when spring has gone and youth has fled,
The maiden and the flowers will soon be dead."

Daiyu does die of disappointed love in the end, and there is a poignant deathbed scene in which she burns all her poetry. Her literary bent marked her as a girl of unusual refinement and education. It was not uncommon for girls in upper-class homes to be tutored with their brothers, but while Daiyu had studied the classics, her girl cousins could barely read or write. This did her no harm in the rather elevated ambience of the Jia household, where couplets etched on wooden boards urging "the jewel of learning" to shine "more effulgently than the sun and moon" could be found decorating the halls. Society might not have approved of unconventional behaviour in women, but in more rarefied circles it could certainly accommodate a degree of eccentricity. Some possibilities existed for women alongside the traditional roles of daughter, wife and mother. A woman could be mildly intellectual or accomplished without inviting censure, and enthusiasms of a genteel sort, be they for literature, calligraphy or music, could be indulged in with perfect propriety.

Chinese notions of ideal womanhood were moulded by both tradition and works of fiction, and Lin Daiyu will always be seen as one model: the well-bred maiden who is sensitive and cultivated and, above all, faithful. Another prevailing image, a negative one, is the *femme fatale* whose sexual allure wreaks dire consequences on those who fall prey to it.

If seductive charms are associated with danger, one reason is the example of a few women in history who catapulted themselves to power and brought about the ruin of empires through manipulating men's weakness for a lovely face or a beautiful body. Several imperial favourites have had such a grip on the popular imagination. One of them, the Empress Dowager Cixi, is viewed as an exemplar of licentiousness, ambition and vanity. A favourite concubine of Emperor Xianfeng, she acquired a taste for meddling in politics and wanted nothing more thereafter than to annex his power for herself. She gained her chance soon enough, for as regent to two boy emperors she became the *de facto* ruler of China for nearly half a century. It was said that she plotted the deaths of several of her opponents. Such wickedness went unpunished, but she was ever afterwards condemned for hurrying the last crumbling years of imperial rule towards its final demise.

The 'dragon ladies' of Chinese history cannot appear in our mind's eye as anything but very beautiful and magnificently dressed. Of course empresses were a cut above the rest, their most formal robe a dazzling creation of golden silk, the fabric itself covered with symbols of nobility, happiness and omnipotence, all meticulously woven or embroidered in skeins of luminous floss. Imperial dragon robes were rivalled by few garments for sumptuousness, their value deriving as much from the costliness of the materials used as the painstaking industry of the many nimble fingers which fashioned them long ago.

Cixi needed no 'symbols of authority' to advertise her hold on the reins of power, though she would have found the occult significance of signs and emblems as compelling as many of her contemporaries. She liked being photographed in robes splattered with felicitous or Buddhist motifs such as clouds (symbolising peace), swastikas (seal of Buddha's heart and an emblem of immortality), butterflies (associated with beauty and marital bliss), bats (representing good fortune) or the stylised character of *shou* (longevity). An observer once described her in a brocade gown of imperial yellow fastened from the right shoulder to the hem with buttons of jade. From the top button hung a string of enormous pearls, while a scent bag with black silk tassels dangled at one side. She affected the long fingernails of the aristocrat and scholar and sheathed

the tips of the third and fourth digits of either hand in nail protectors of jade and gold studded with rubies and pearls. On her feet she wore shoes with six-inch high, stilt-like soles.

Being a Manchu, the Empress Dowager did not totter about on unnaturally tiny feet, but if footbinding was discouraged by the Qing, the Chinese continued to inflict this cruel practice on their daughters until the 20th century. Initially found only among the gentry, bound feet became so widely accepted as a norm of feminine attractiveness that the practice spread even to peasant homes. To deform growing feet in that way, the binding had to begin when the girl was quite young, generally aged five or six. She would have her feet compressed by long strips of cotton cloth until her four minor toes were crushed under the sole. After years of this treatment the arch bones broke and she would be able to hobble only on the heels of her feet, and with difficulty.

We may well wonder why men thought those misshapen feet enticing and erotic. But so tenacious a hold did this strange custom have on the populace that untold suffering was caused to achieve something close to the ideal size. A woman with ugly large feet was assumed to lead a humble life of labour and drudgery rather than an affluent one of leisure, one which would spare a lady from the exertion of walking far and allow her to be carried about daintily ensconced in a sedan chair. No girl would find a good husband, it was asserted, unless her feet were not much longer than three inches, a standard described as a *jin lian* – "golden lotus" or "golden lily". To encase them, gorgeously embroidered shoes were produced, some of them so ornate as to have become collectors' pieces today. But such fetishistic accoutrements merely served to make the whole practice seem more abhorrent and grotesque to Western missionaries, modern thinkers and other campaigners against footbinding in the early 20th century. Few remained unaware of the saying, "For every pair of golden lilies there is a vat of tears".

They also railed against the male domination implied, for bound feet restricted movement, confining women to their imprisoning courtyard and keeping them dependent and submissive. "Buried in the women's quarters," lamented a poet, "The days pass in idleness." In old China a woman was subject to her father first of all and, on being wed, to her husband and mother-in-law. Marriage, considered the only proper career for a young woman, was not so much made in heaven as arranged by matchmaking parents. Alliances were based not on love but on common family interests, not to mention the size of the dowry. Sometimes the couples were strangers to each other until their engagement, or even their wedding day. After marriage, a woman's status improved only if she gave birth to a son; if she did not, her husband might take a concubine if he could afford one and leave his jilted wife to suffer in silence.

A girl's reputation for purity was, of course, vital and strenuously defended. This was done not only by the imposition of a strict moral and social code but also by customs such as footbinding, all of which limited contacts with men other than husbands and close relatives. During the most reactionary period of the Qing dynasty, when pressures on observing traditional rules of behaviour were particularly intense, women actually connived at their own subjugation, going to absurd lengths to demonstrate their faithfulness and chastity. Betrothed girls whose fiancés died before their wedding would insist on remaining virgins for life, while widows either committed suicide or, at the very least, refused to remarry, thus inspiring a huge number of memorial arches to be erected in honour of their constancy and virtue. It was no wonder that as the dynasty drew to its close, one phenomenon making itself felt should be the growing demand for females to be given equal rights. Even for women of the elite, the prospect of emancipation was too irresistible for their privileged but cruelly confined world to endure.

The paintings in these pages are witness to the Western vogue for chinoiserie *in the late 18th and early 19th century, when illustrations of an exotic China and its people proliferated, many of them portraits of Chinese women rendered with a vivid palette.*

Hair ornaments, particularly pins inlaid with kingfisher feathers, were one of the main forms of personal adornment. (From left to right) A floral arrangement; a multi-colour butterfly; and a butterfly with gold filigree.

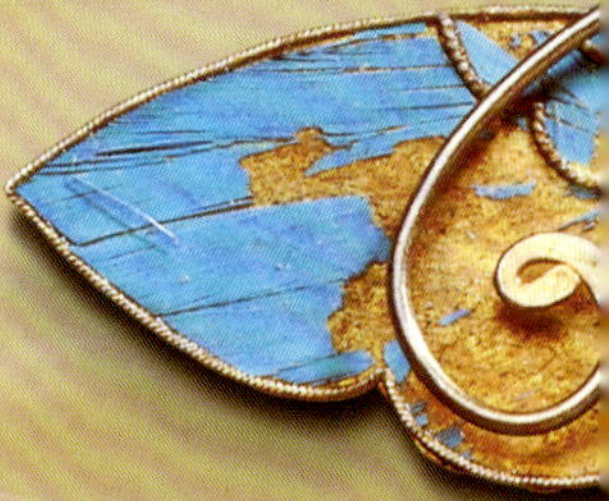

Shaped as flowering branches and leaves, these hairpins are decorated with kingfisher feathers, silver-gilt filigree, jade and semi-precious stones.

Hair ornaments. Bats were a popular motif (right and below), as were peonies. The one on the left of the two studded with semi-precious stones incorporates the Chinese character for "longevity".

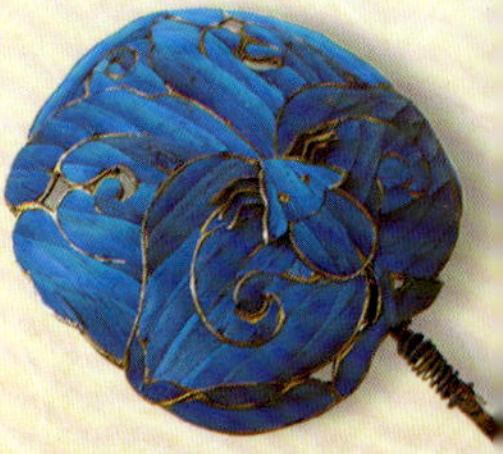

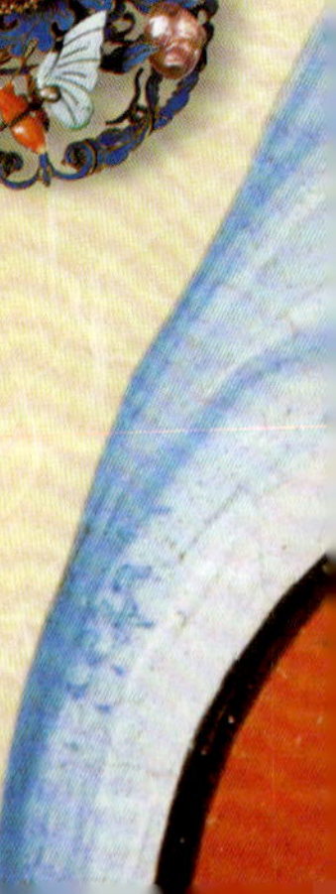

Wood and ivory combs, and a toilet box with mirror in which combs would have been kept.

Paintings showing the minutiae of Chinese life set in precisely observed interiors of houses, courtyards or gardens, including scenes of eating or serving tea, were much in demand.

Designs of fish, foliage and birds in relief combine with openwork to decorate a ball-shaped fragrance locket; coral and jade embellish two small ornaments; and a child's silver padlock bears the inscription "Prolong years and increase longevity".

Two of these silver pendants and lockets with chased detail are further embellished with dangling beads.

Precious and semi-precious stones and openwork have all been used to stunning effect in these pieces of jewellery.

Bangles and bracelets, including one with coral beads and two inlaid with turquoise.

In this interior scene, where a small garden may be seen at rear framed by intricate casements, three women are playing a board game. An attendant is just coming into the hall with tea.

Bats, a mystic knot and tassels ornament the frame of this kimono mirror with a lady's portrait painted on the back.

Set of Chinese kimono mirrors, their backs decorated with carved and painted ivory inlay (left); portraits of ladies (centre); and picture of lady at a writing desk (right).

Delicately filigreed ivory kimono mirrors enamel painted at the back with portraits of women, some showing elaborate hairstyles. Two of the mirrors (left and centre) are framed in tortoiseshell.

This ornately embroidered cream silk and tasselled umbrella has an ivory knob at the tip and a finely carved ivory handle. (Inset) Small hand mirror painted with the figure of a lady.

Lady with a fan was a favourite theme of China trade paintings. In such portraits, the women's faces rarely have any individuality, but the figures are always resplendently clad and adorned.

Imperial yellow formal robe with dragons and the twelve symbols of authority. (Following pages) Detail showing the five-clawed dragon chasing the pearl of wisdom.

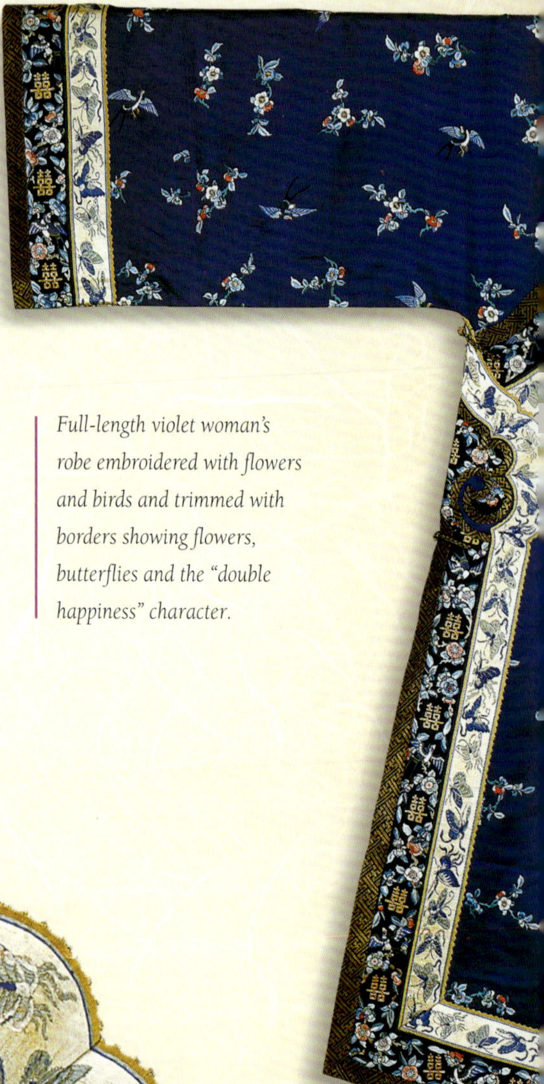

Full-length violet woman's robe embroidered with flowers and birds and trimmed with borders showing flowers, butterflies and the "double happiness" character.

Detail of a painting showing two women in a courtyard.

Short formal robe, richly patterned with satin-stitch and Peking knot-stitch embroidery and trimmed with an auspicious design of deer, lotus, crane and flowers.

Woman's wedding robe with multi-coloured embroidered sleeve bands. (Inset) This scent purse, with flowers embroidered in running stitch and a jade bead threaded into the tassel, might have been part of a trousseau.

A baizi (hundred-children) motif was often seen on women's robes; this one is set off with sumptuous gold-couched and embroidered sleeve bands.

Turquoise robe embroidered all over with peony, phoenix, peacock and rhino horn motifs in Peking knot-stitch. The green scarf with tassels is delicately embroidered with birds and flowers.

Woman's robe with cream, yellow, blue and pink trimming embroidered in a pattern of clouds. (Inset) The rectangular shaped purse is decorated with embroidery and coloured tassels.

Formal woman's robe, the plain cream sleeve bands in striking contrast to the elaborate border and collar embroidery depicting a garden scene. (Inset) Gold-couched kidney-shaped purse.

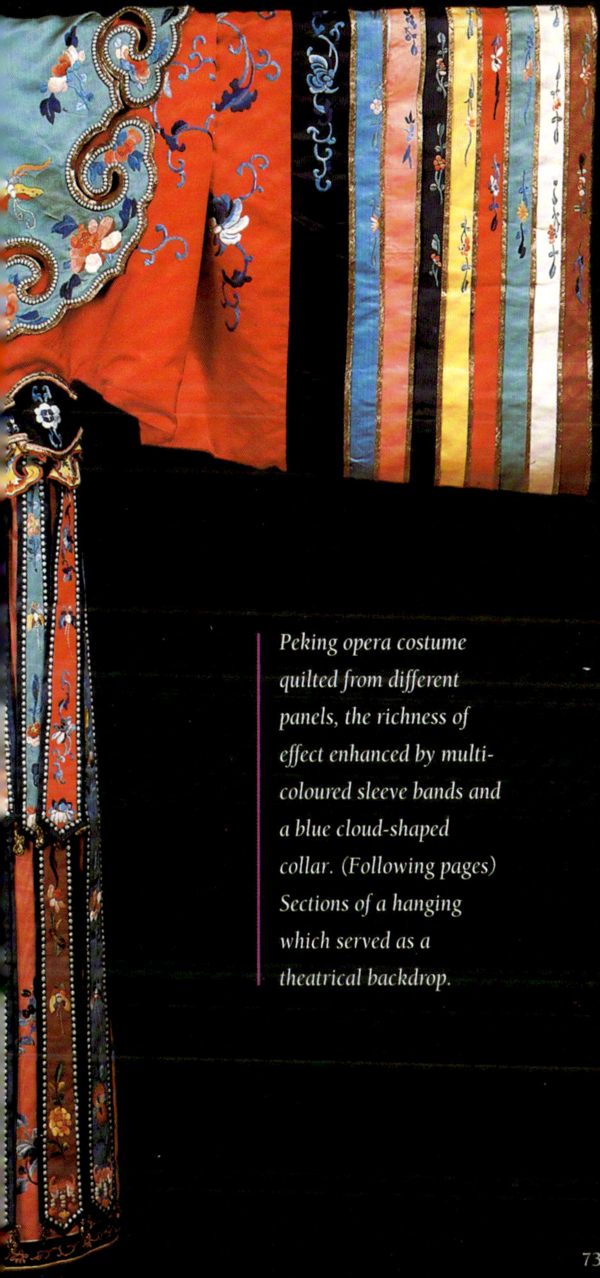

Peking opera costume quilted from different panels, the richness of effect enhanced by multi-coloured sleeve bands and a blue cloud-shaped collar. (Following pages) Sections of a hanging which served as a theatrical backdrop.

Taught to embroider from an early age, girls would lavish their needlework skills on shoes, the smaller the better, according to the fashion of the day. Hours were spent decorating them with motifs symbolising harmony and fertility.

(Foreground) Shoes for bound feet embroidered with flowers. (Top left) Couched in gold and embroidered, this shoe has a metal-studded wooden sole. (Top right) Purple small-heeled shoes.

(Top) Shoes embroidered with flowers, fish and geometric patterns, their tops trimmed with velvet brocade. (Bottom) Black satin uppers on a shaped sole trimmed with ribbon. (Left) Gouache painting on rice paper of a lady playing a stringed instrument.

A collection of bound-foot shoes showing a range of styles, colours and decorative elements.
(Top) A northern style incorporating rounded supporting heels.
(Centre) Bed slippers.
(Bottom) The trimming on this heavily embroidered shoe includes a decorative butterfly.

A life of refinement could be passed cultivating literary pursuits from which women were not excluded if they felt so inclined. This one is portrayed with the paraphernalia of a scholar's table, including scroll, brushes and inkstand.

(Clockwise) Blue and white ceramic brush washer in the shape of a slipper; ivory brush pot carved in high relief; white ceramic brush pointer; blue and white ceramic water dropper in the form of a rooster; porcelain brush rest.

Paintings like this one, of docile women gathered behind a carved balustrade, perpetuated the image of feminine grace and delicacy but also hinted at their confined lives.

Paper fans stiffened by lacquer sticks and gorgeously painted with vignettes of gardens, flowers and emblems.

(Clockwise from top left) Lacquer box; fan painted with a floral motif; embroidered fan case; ivory-stick fan with vignettes of landscape, dwellings, boats and figures.

This fan supported with pierced and carved red ivory sticks and spliced over by paper is painted with floral-bordered scenes. A detail appears on the right.

Folding fan with red and green stained ivory sticks. The multitude of figures is painted on the paper leaf in gouache.

(Left) Paper fan stiffened by carved bamboo sticks; the painting is of figures in a garden among deer and butterflies. (Right) Detail from the scene of a lady holding a lantern.

Folding fan supported by ivory stick guards, the paper painted in watercolour showing landscape with mountain, trees, stream and figures. (Inset) Fan cases.

Octagonal silk hand-screen, its front depicting figures in a garden clustered round the moon hare, and its reverse painted with a pair of butterflies amid peonies and prunus, has edges bound in brocade. The ivory handle is decorated with carvings of plum blossom.

This makes a pair with the hand-screen on the previous page. Women at leisure, a pavilion, an ornamental pond, mandarin ducks and children playing make for a delightful scene. Butterflies on stems of peonies and daisies are painted on the reverse.

This group of performers allowed the artist to illustrate the variety of Chinese musical instruments, both wind and stringed. Rich families sometimes retained troupes of musicians and actors for private performances of opera to celebrate birthdays or festivals.